GEORGE,
the DRAGON and the PRINCESS

CHRIS WORMELL

RED FOX

Far, far away over the high, high mountains,

in an old castle wall, in a tiny, tiny hole . . .

there lived a little mouse called George.

Now George, despite the sign above his hole,

was not dangerous or fierce at all.

In fact, he was rather timid . . .

and clumsy, too!

He was always trapping his tail in
the deckchair.

And he was hopeless at lighting fires.

And if he did get a fire going, he was bound
to burn his cheese on toast.

Poor George was hopeless at most things.

But there was one small thing he could do . . .

actually, it was quite a big thing . . .

He could scare dragons!

Well, he could scare *this* dragon.

Because *this* dragon was terrified of mice!

The princess turned out to be brilliant
at making cheese on toast.

She made extra-large portions, so George
could eat as much as he liked . . .

and he did!

To Lucy, Laura and Chantelle

GEORGE, THE DRAGON AND THE PRINCESS
A RED FOX BOOK 978 1 862 30833 6

First published in Great Britain by Jonathan Cape,
an imprint of Random House Children's Books
A Random House Group Company

Jonathan Cape edition published 2007
Red Fox edition published 2008
This edition with CD published 2009

1 3 5 7 9 10 8 6 4 2

Red Fox Books are published by Random House Children's Books,
61-63 Uxbridge Road, London W5 5SA

www.kidsatrandomhouse.co.uk
www.rbooks.co.uk

Addresses for companies within The Random House Group Limited can be found at:
www.randomhouse.co.uk/offices.htm

THE RANDOM HOUSE GROUP Limited Reg. No. 954009

A CIP catalogue record for this book is available from the British Library.

Printed in China